LORAINE'S
HOUSE

W9-AWZ-171

Barbara M. Joosse

GHOST TRAP

A WILD WILLIE MYSTERY

Illustrated by Sue Truesdell

Clarion Books

New York

Clarion Books
a Houghton Mifflin Company imprint
215 Park Avenue South, New York, NY 10003
Text copyright © 1998 by Barbara M. Joosse
Illustrations copyright © 1998 by Sue Truesdell

The interior illustrations for this book were executed in pen and
ink with ink washes on Arches cold press watercolor paper.

The text was set in 14/19-point Palatino.

Printed in the U.S.A.

Joosse, Barbara M.
    Ghost trap: a Wild Willie mystery / by Barbara M. Joosse ;
illustrated by Sue Truesdell.
        p.   cm.
        Summary: When Wild Willie's best friend Kyle moves back to the
    neighborhood the boys suspect that Kyle's new house is haunted.
        ISBN 0-395-66587-6
        [1. Best friends—Fiction.   2. Moving, Househould—Fiction.
3. Detectives—Fiction.   4. Ghosts—Fiction.   5. Parrots—Fiction.]
I. Truesdell, Sue, ill.   II. Title.
PZ7.J7435Gh   1998
[E]—dc21   97-22655
                                                       CIP
                                                       AC

MP 10 9 8 7 6 5

To my hero, Don
Also to the other Sunset Court Kids
Thanks for picking skunk cabbage.
—Witch Hazel
B.M.J.

For Joe
S.T.

Contents

Oh, Wild Willie!

It was the beginning of the weekend and I didn't have any homework. Lucy and I were sitting on my front porch, drinking orange soda through bendable straws. I had a pocket full of poppers—those little firecrackers you throw at the sidewalk.

"What do you want to do?" I asked, throwing some poppers.

"Definitely camping." Lucy threw some poppers, too. "I want to sleep outside in a sleeping bag."

"After that we can look through people's garbage to see what good stuff they're throwing away, " I said.

"And blast our bikes through leaves in the gutters, " Lucy said.

"Together," I said.

"Of course," she said.

Yup. The weekend looked perfect . . . and I didn't know it, but the best part was coming up. As Lucy and I threw some more poppers, we saw a horse and a guy in an actual cowboy outfit stop in front of my house (and I'm not kidding about this). The guy walked up the porch steps. "Howdy," he said. "Are you Wild Willie?"

"Yes," I said.

"I'm Tex, from the Buckaroo Singing Telegram Company, and I have a message for you."

"Wow!" I said. "A singing telegram?"

"It's from Kyle Krane of Cleveland, Ohio."

"The King!" I said. Kyle used to live next door, but then he moved to stupid-Cleveland-stupid-Ohio and Lucy's family moved into his house.

Tex began to strum his old guitar to the tune of "Oh, Susanna."

(strum strum)
"It rained all night the day I left
the weather it was dry,
the sun so hot I froze to death
Wild Willie don't you cry.

(strum strum)
Oh, Wild Willie, oh don't you cry
fer me
'cause I went to stupid Cleve-a-land
with my whole family.

I'm tellin' you in this here song
instead of a dumb letter.
We're gettin' outa Cleve-a-land
'cause we like Grafton better.

Oh, Wild Willie, oh don't you cry
fer me
fer I'm movin' back to Sunset Court,
ain't that right neighborly?"
(*strum-a-strum-strum*)

"Yow! Did you hear that, Lucy? Kyle's moving back to the neighborhood!"

"Sounds like it," said Lucy.

"Well now, partner, I gotta mosey on down to the next job," said Tex. He swept his cowboy hat off his head and bowed. "So long," he said. Then Tex got up on his horse and rode away. Just like in the movies.

I did a cowboy dance and sang the "Oh, Wild Willie" song.

"My old best friend is coming back!" I yelled. I reached into my pocket and pulled out a whole bunch of poppers. I threw them at the sidewalk. *Pop pop pop pop pop.*

I was so happy I didn't notice Lucy

wasn't singing or dancing or yelling or popping. She was real quiet.

Pop

My First Best Friend

I was way excited. Kyle was my first best friend. Before he moved away, we did everything together. We planted a salad garden, we built airplanes out of the swing set, we mixed gross food together, we played baseball. Now he was coming back! Now everything was going to be like before.

Except, of course, Kyle was going to live in a new house, two blocks away. Lucy was living in his old house, next door to me.

Lucy and I waited on the sidewalk for Kyle's family, in front of his new house. "This is going to be great! This is going to be great!" I kept saying.

Lucy kept not saying anything.

Finally I saw their car. *"King Kyle!"* I yelled when I saw his good old face.

Kyle burst out of the car and jumped on me. We rolled around on the ground, socking each other, grinning like crazy

guys . . . just like before he moved away.

"This is the best!" he sighed, putting his arm around me.

"This is the greatest," I sighed, putting my arm around my old best friend.

"A-HEM!" said Lucy.

I forgot Lucy. I forgot she'd never even *seen* Kyle before. "Hello, Kyle," she said with thin lips. Then she walked up to my other arm and stuck herself under it.

Kyle's mom rushed up to us while his dad unlocked the front door. "Willie!" she said, giving me a kiss. She had lipstick on. "Oh, sweetie, it's so good to see you. Kyle sure missed his best friend, but now the two of you are back together. And this must be Lucy."

While Kyle's mom was busy looking at Lucy, I wiped off her kiss.

"Well now, I'm dying to see the inside of our new house," said Kyle's mom. "Aren't you? Come on!"

Kyle, Lucy, and I walked to the house, arm-in-arm. It felt funny walking that way. Kyle stepped up when Lucy stepped down and I was yanked around in the middle. Then we got to the doorway.

"We can't fit through with three of us," said Lucy. "Only two."

Kyle looked at Lucy with bullet-eyes, and then he looked at me. Lucy looked at Kyle with arrow-eyes, and then she tapped her foot.

Yow! Was I supposed to pick? If I walked with Lucy, Kyle would be angry. If I walked with Kyle, Lucy would be. Luckily, we heard a bloodcurdling scream coming from the living room. We let go of each other and ran in. There were Kyle's parents, looking like they'd seen a ghost. But there wasn't a ghost, only . . .

"Holy cow!" said Kyle, his eyes big as soccer balls.

"Look at this!" I said, my jaw dropping to my knees.

"Some place!" said Lucy.

◆ 3 ◆

Secret Passage

"Oh my, oh my, oh my!" Kyle's mom kept saying. She was staring at the same thing we were staring at: The whole living room looked like a police station. One wall was a giant bulletin board, and it was full of newspaper articles about unsolved crimes. There was a big metal desk in one corner, and it had an official name-thing on it: Loraine Lamonde, Detective. Next to that was a chalkboard with lists.

Kyle's dad shook his head. "They said this was a handyman's special, but I had no idea."

"Oh my, oh my, oh my," said Kyle's mom.

"This is the coolest place I've ever seen! Look at this great stuff," said Kyle, opening the desk drawers. "There's writing pads and newspaper articles and *Real Crime* magazines in here."

"Lucky dog," I said.

"What are we going to do?" asked Kyle's mom. "This place is a mess!"

"The moving van won't be here till Saturday," said Kyle's dad. "We can have everything out by then."

"But Dad!" Kyle said. "Can't we keep—"

Kyle's mom had this *in-one-minute-I'm-going-to-cry* look and Kyle's dad had this *don't-mess-with-me-young-man* look, so I yanked Kyle and Lucy out of there, into the dining room.

"Why are they going to get rid of that cool stuff?" Kyle asked.

"It's like fish and candy bars," Lucy said. "Kids like candy bars. Grownups like fish. You can't explain it."

Then we walked up the creaky stairs, to look at Kyle's bedroom.

"Was Loraine Lamonde a detective?" asked Lucy. Because Lucy was still a new kid in town, she didn't know all the good stuff about the neighbors yet.

"Maybe," I said, brushing a cobweb off my face. "But she never left her house."

"Mom said my room would be the first one on the right," said Kyle, putting his hand on the doorknob.

"Wonder what's in there?" asked Lucy.

"Maybe spy stuff. Maybe a dead body," I said.

Kyle opened the door. "Phooey. It's just regular bedroom stuff," he said. "A bed and a dresser and lamps."

Kyle and I looked in the dresser and Lucy went into the closet.

"Wow!" she said, her voice muffled. "This is the biggest closet I've ever seen. Really big." I headed for the closet when suddenly Lucy appeared in the bedroom doorway.

"Hey!" said Kyle. "Weren't you just inside the closet?"

"I was, but now I'm here!" she said. Lucy was way excited. "I got here through the *secret passage in the closet!*"

Kyle and I almost knocked each other over getting to the closet door. It was dark in there but when my eyes got used to the darkness I could see a crack of light coming from somewhere farther away. We followed the light. At the end was another bedroom.

"Let's do it again!" cried Kyle.

The three of us grabbed each other's hands and felt along the wall. We walked slowly and we didn't say anything. I could hear Kyle and Lucy breathing. Before we got to the other bedroom, I felt an opening in the wall. "Feel here," I whispered.

"It's another passage!" Kyle whispered back. "Come on!" He started leading the way.

Lucy squeezed in front of him. "I found the passage," she said. "I should lead."

Kyle shoved in front of Lucy. "But this

18

is my house. And this is *my* secret passage. I get to lead."

Kyle and Lucy were fighting so much they bumped into something. "Ow!" Lucy said.

"Somebody put stairs in here," said Kyle, rubbing his leg.

Lucy and Kyle shoved their way up the stairs. "Yow!" said Lucy. "Up here's . . ."

"The attic!" said Kyle, interrupting her. "And it's in *my* house."

Kyle started pacing around the attic. "This is the best attic I've ever seen. It's full of junk. Old TVs and old-fashioned record players. We could make inventions out of this junk for the rest of our lives and still have stuff left."

As Kyle walked, there was this little crunching sound beneath his feet. He bent down and picked something up off the floor. "Birdseed," he said. "The floor's full of it."

"Look! There's tons of it piled in bags along the wall," I said.

"Loraine Lamonde must have been a bird lover," said Kyle.

"Probably fed them all winter," said Lucy. "But I wonder why there's a secret passage?"

"And why all her stuff was left in the house." Kyle said.

"*I'm* going to find out," said Lucy.

We were so busy talking, we didn't pay any attention to a very soft noise that came from the corner of the attic.

◆ 4 ◆

Loony Loraine

The next morning, I was still in my pajamas when I heard a knock on my bedroom window.

"Friend or foe?" I asked.

"Kyle," came the voice.

I opened my window and King Kyle crawled in.

"Hey," he said, stretching out on my bed. "We can finally have some privacy. Lucy's probably doing girl stuff."

"Lucy doesn't do girl stuff," I said. "She's not a girly girl, she's a sporty girl."

"*All* girls are girly girls," said Kyle.

I just shrugged. Let Kyle find out for himself about Lucy.

"But here's what I came over to tell you! A weird thing happened last night. I was in my bed, and suddenly I heard . . ."

Ping. Ping. Ping.

"What was that?" asked Kyle. His face got real white.

"Stones. Lucy throws them at my window when she wants to come in." I opened the window.

Lucy crawled in, carrying our official detective notebook. "You won't believe what I . . . Oh. Hello, Kyle." Icicles dripped from her words.

"Hello, Lucille," said Kyle. Icicles dripped from his words.

Lucy flipped open her notebook. "I interviewed some of your neighbors about Loraine Lamonde yesterday. Wait'll you hear this!"

"I bet she was pretty ordinary," said
Kyle, "and she died in her sleep in a nurs-
ing home. From old age."

"No!" said Lucy. "She wasn't ordinary
and she died at home!"

"Jeez," said Kyle. His face got even whiter, like all the blood was sucked out. "I forgot I have to . . . uh . . . clean my room. Gotta go." And he did.

"You've got a weird friend there, Willie," said Lucy. "Anyway, let me tell you what I found out.

"First, Loraine was a mystery freak. Kyle's next-door neighbor, Mrs. Krantz, said she watched detective shows on TV, day and night. She said Loraine was a tube boob, and I quote, 'She played that darned tube so loud she woke the dead.' Harry, the mailman, said he delivered gobs of detective magazines to her house."

"Was she a real detective?" I asked.

"Mrs. Krantz said she was an amateur detective, not a police one."

"Like us," I said.

"The only thing that was pretty weird is that she was a hermit—that's why people called her Loony Loraine. She kept her window shades drawn and never went out. She made phone orders of all the things she needed, like groceries and hardware, and had them delivered. The only people she saw face to face were the delivery people and Mrs. Krantz."

"What about all that birdseed? Did anybody say she liked birds?"

Lucy flipped through her notebook

pages. "Nope. Nobody mentioned any-thing about birds."

"But why would anyone leave all that stuff inside the house?" I asked.

"Here's what I got," said Lucy, flipping a notebook page again. "The only relative Loony Loraine had was a greedy nephew, Neil. Mrs. Krantz said Neil got all her money when she died. He was in a real hurry to get it, too, so he sold the house without bothering to clean it up. She's only been dead a few weeks!"

"Wow! You said she died at home?"

"Yes," said Lucy. "Mrs. Krantz suspected something was wrong because she hadn't heard the TV for several days. Mrs. Krantz called, but there was no answer, so she phoned the police. Inside the house they found her dead body. Guess the exact spot she died."

"Her detective desk?"

"No. *She died in Kyle's bedroom!*"

♦ 5 ♦

Aren't Ghosts Just Pretend?

It had been a week since Kyle moved back—a weird week. Here's what had happened since then:

1. We explored Kyle's new house, including the detective stuff *and* the secret passage.
2. Lucy investigated Loony Loraine.
3. Kyle stopped speaking to Lucy.
4. Lucy stopped speaking to Kyle.

So now it was Saturday morning and I was watching cartoons. By myself. The first two shows were pretty good. The third one looked like the first two so I watched it upside down. The fourth one looked like the third and first so I watched it with green plastic over the screen. That's when Mom came in.

"Hi, sweetie," she said. She looked at the TV. "I see you have on the green channel. Anything interesting?"

"No," I said. "Cartoon shows aren't as fun as they used to be."

"Mmmm," Mom said. "That's one of the symptoms of cartoonhead."

"Cartoonhead isn't a real thing. It's what you say when I watch too much TV."

"Exactly," said Mom. "It's a beautiful day! Why aren't you outside with Kyle and Lucy?"

"When I'm with Kyle, Lucy gets mad.

When I'm with Lucy, Kyle gets mad. I'm better off in here."

"It sound like a Friend War. Kyle wants things to be the way they were before Lucy moved here. Lucy wants things to be the way they were before Kyle moved back. Both of them want to be your best friend."

"Yeah," I said.

"So now you're trying to keep everybody happy. The problem is, when you do that, *nobody's* happy. It's like dinner. Dad likes steak, but not vegetables. You like pizza, but not meat. I like vegetables. If I tried to please everyone, we'd eat three separate meals. So sometimes I make steak, sometimes vegetarian spaghetti, sometimes pizza with eggplant. See?"

"No," I said. "Talk regular."

"Don't worry so much about making people happy. Be a good friend to Kyle, and a good friend to Lucy, and let them work things out themselves."

"Right," I said, and then Mom left.

It's been a long time since Mom was a kid. She forgot how it was. Her advice always sounds good, but it doesn't really work. If I did what she said, *nobody* would be my friend.

I went into the back yard and lay on the ground. I covered myself up with leaves until nothing was sticking out. I decided to stay in there a long time. Maybe I

wouldn't come out for lunch. Maybe not
even dinner. Especially if Mom made
pizza with eggplant on it.

"Hey, Willie," came Kyle's voice.

"How did you know where I was?" I
asked.

"I watched you from the sidewalk. Can I come in?" Kyle didn't wait for my answer. He crawled into the leaves and covered up.

"How are things?" I asked him, from my side of the pile.

"Not so good," said Kyle. "I don't like Lucy very much. She's too bossy."

"She is bossy," I said. "But she's fun. Maybe you'll like her after a while."

"I'll never like her," said Kyle. "She's a girl. But that's not all. It's my house."

"You want your old house back?"

"No, I just want *out* of the one we moved into. It's haunted."

"What?"

"I'm not kidding, Willie. There's a ghost in my house."

I stuck my head out of the leaves. "A real ghost? Are you sure? I like ghosts . . . in movies. But I'm not sure I'd really like to see one. Besides, aren't ghosts just pretend? Aren't they just Halloween costumes?"

"Shhhhh! It might hear you."

"What?" I whispered. "Did it follow you? Is it here right now?"

"I don't know," said Kyle. "I'm not a ghost expert. I didn't believe in ghosts either . . . until now.

I reached through the leaves and squeezed Kyle's arm. "How do you know it's a real ghost?"

"I just know," said Kyle. "That's why I want you to come over."

"You mean *now?*"

"Yes!" said Kyle.

♦ 6 ♦

Whose Best Friend Are You, Anyway?

On the way to his house, King Kyle said, "When we go up to my room, be real quiet. Don't talk and don't step on the middle of the steps because they're creaky. We don't want the ghost to hear."

"What should we do when we get to your room?" I asked.

"Sit on my bed. Be quiet. Listen. You'll see what I mean."

Kyle opened the front door very slowly. We walked on tiptoes to the stairs. Then

we walked on the edge of the staircase so it wouldn't creak.

When we got to Kyle's room we sat on the bed and waited.

At first, waiting was fun. Scary fun. But then I felt itchy. Slowly I reached for an itch, but as soon as I got it, another place itched. Just when I was ready to explode with itches, I heard it. *Rustle rustle rustle.* Kyle pointed to the closet and the secret passage. The sound was coming from there. My heart was thundering like a locomotive but I guess the ghost didn't hear that because then it spoke.

"Loraine! Loraine!"

Kyle's eyes got so big I thought they'd fall right out of the sockets. I figured mine looked like that, too. Then it spoke again.

"Gotcha, Scarface."

I grabbed Kyle, my old buddy, my first best friend in all the world. We were going to run for it when his bedroom door burst open.

"Aaaaaaaugh!" we both screamed.

It was Lucy.

"What's the matter? You look like you've seen a ghost or something."

"We di—" I started to say, but Kyle jabbed me in my side with his elbow.

"I was looking all over for you, Willie," said Lucy. "We have a soccer game in an hour."

Soccer sounded really good just then, so I started to get up from the bed. But Kyle grabbed my arm and pulled me back.

"He can't go," Kyle said.

"Why not?" asked Lucy.

"Because we're busy."

"Doing what?"

I started to say, "Listening for . . ." but Kyle slapped a hand over my mouth. He whispered in my ear, "I don't want her to know about the ghost. It's our thing."

"Whispering in front of someone is not very nice," said Lucy. "And besides,

whatever you're listening for, it can't be as
important as a soccer game."

"Excuse me," said Kyle. "Soccer is just a
game. *This* is life and death."

Lucy folded her arms in front of her
chest and shouted, "*Whose friend are you
anyway, Willie? Kyle's or mine? Soccer or sitting in some stuffy old room . . . listening?*"

Kyle shouted, too. "*He was my friend
first!*"

"*But he's my friend now!*"

"*Wait!*" I yelled. "This is so stupid I can't believe it! We've got a real, live mystery here and we can't even solve it because you're fighting."

"*Braaaaaaaaack!*"

"What was that?" asked Lucy.

"A ghost," said Kyle. "Let's get out of here!"

Like Bubble Gum

We ran like the wind, out of the bedroom, down the stairs, out of the haunted house, down two blocks to my house, and dove into the pile of leaves. We were gasping. We were sweating. We were scared stiff. We were having the time of our lives.

Finally, Lucy spoke. "What ghost?" We were buried in leaves and I couldn't see her. I could only hear her voice.

"Loony Loraine," I said, in a shaky voice.

"She's haunting my house," said Kyle, from beneath a trembling pile of leaves.

"She actually *talks*, Lucy!" I said. She says her name, Loraine, and I heard her say, 'Gotcha Scarface!'"

"Scarface?" Lucy said.

We stuck our heads out of the leaves and Kyle said, "She says lots of stuff. Her name, but also, 'Release your weapons,' 'Get outa my face,' and 'Book 'em.' Stuff like that."

"Wow, that's exactly the kind of thing Loraine would say," said Lucy. "She was an amateur detective."

"Do ghosts ever hurt you?" Kyle asked.

"They can scare you, but how could they hurt you? They're made of cloud-stuff or smoke or something. They don't have real bodies. Loraine must be trying to scare you out of her house, that's all. She was a hermit, remember, and she's probably shy," said Lucy.

"She doesn't sound shy," I said.

"A lot of shy people sound bossy, but they're mushy inside," said Lucy. "It's all a bluff."

Like Lucy and Kyle, I thought. Bossy outside, mushy inside. I wondered if they'd ever get that. At least now they were talking to each other.

"What other clues do you have?" asked Lucy.

"A whispering sound," said Kyle. "Like this. *Rustle rustle rustle.* Like a ghost moving."

"The voice and rustling came from the secret passage," I said. "So Loraine's ghost must live in there."

"See what I mean? She's shy," said Lucy. "She doesn't want to come out where you can see her."

"But I want to see her, " Kyle said, "at least I think I do. What if I see her and she's headless or bloody? Or what if I can't get rid of her and she haunts me forever? Or what if she *can* hurt me and . . ."

"If she tries to hurt you, she'll have to deal with me, too," I said.

"And me!" said Lucy.

"Then we'll stick together?" asked Kyle.

"Like bubble gum to a hot sidewalk," said Lucy.

Could it be true? Were Lucy and Kyle starting to be friends?

"You know," said Lucy. "I don't know one single person who's ever seen a ghost. We'd be the first. We'd be famous."

"And maybe rich. We could get our picture in the paper and be on talk shows. Talk shows pay a lot of money," said Kyle.

"If we go to the newspapers, they'll just think we're little kids and don't know anything," I said.

"You're right," said Lucy. "We need proof."

"Do you have a plan?" asked Kyle.

I said, "Part of a plan. The part I have is this: We hide in Kyle's bedroom and wait. When the ghost comes out, we jump out and *take her picture.* Then we have proof."

"You're diabolical, Willie!" said Lucy.

I like it when Lucy says I'm diabolical—clever and rotten at the same time.

"But Lucy's right," said Kyle. "Loraine must be shy. I've never seen her, just heard her. What makes you think she'll come out?"

"Okay, okay," I said. "I didn't say I had the *whole* plan figured out, just part of it. Are we a detective agency or not?"

"Willie's right," said Kyle. "We can figure this out together. We're a team."

The Plan

I always figure things out better when I'm eating. So the three of us went inside to the kitchen and I got out salted peanuts-in-a-shell and put them on the table.

Lucy pulled out the official agency notebook. "Let's get started," she said, flipping it open. "Willie's part of the plan is good. We need to take pictures. Does anybody have a camera?"

"I do," said Kyle.

"Good," said Lucy. She wrote *Things to*

Bring on the top of the page, and under it, *Camera—Kyle.* "Now, how are we going to get Loraine to come out?"

Kyle cracked open a peanut. "We need bait, something that'll tempt her out."

"Yeah. Something she can't resist," I said.

"Like what?" Kyle said. "Ghosts don't eat anything. They don't even drink anything. At least, I don't think so."

Lucy started hopping around like a crazy person. "I have it! I have it!" she cried. "This isn't just *any* ghost, it's Loraine. She was an amateur detective. What's the thing a detective can't resist?"

"A crime," I said.

"A dead body!" yelled Kyle.

"Yes!" we said together.

"I'll be the dead body!" Kyle said. "I'll pretend someone put poison in my glass. I'm excellent at dying."

Lucy wrote down *Dead Body and Glass*

of Water — Kyle. "Okay. I'll watch for her through Willie's periscope. When she comes out to inspect the body, I'll throw a blanket over her—to trap her," said Lucy. She wrote down:

Blanket — Lucy.
Periscope — Willie.

"And I'll be ready with the camera," I said. "As soon as you take the blanket off, I'll snap her picture."

"We'll do it when it's dark outside," said Lucy. "Ghosts like the dark." She wrote down *Flashlights — Everyone.*

"Perfect," said Kyle.

"Three minds are sure better than one," Lucy said.

We stuffed peanuts in our pockets for later. I opened the last peanut in the dish. Inside the shell was a triple-nut peanut. Three peanuts in a shell. Like us. I figured it was a good sign.

Ghost Slime

We met in front of Kyle's house. There was a full moon. The wind whipped leaves at us, and the branches rattled their bones. It was the end of October, getting close to Halloween. And we were going to trap a ghost! This was the creepiest, most fun thing I'd ever done in my whole life, and I was doing it with my two best friends.

We tiptoed up the creaky stairs and stood in front of the door to Kyle's room.

I snuck in first and hid behind Kyle's dresser with the camera. Lucy hid behind the chair with the blanket and periscope. Then Kyle walked in with a glass of water.

"Boy, things sure have been creepy lately," Kyle said, loud enough for the ghost to hear. "I keep thinking *someone is following me*. And yesterday, *a car almost hit me*. It's almost like *someone's trying to kill me!*" Kyle took a sip of water. "Yow! This water

sure tastes funny. Sort of like poi—" He grabbed his throat, made a choking sound and let the glass drop to the floor. As he lurched forward, collapsing on the bed, some of the peanuts spilled out of his pockets.

Kyle lay still like a corpse. The bait. We didn't move a muscle. We didn't make a sound. Boy, I really, *really* had to go to the bathroom. I always do when I'm scared.

Suddenly, *zwooooosh!* A gray shape came out of nowhere and headed right for Kyle!

"Gonna get some!" it screamed.

Yowzer!

Lucy crashed out of her hiding place, leaped on the bed, and whipped the blanket through the air like a net.

"Help!" Kyle yelled through the blanket. "It bit me!"

"Brraaaaaugh! Brraaaaaugh!" the ghost screeched.

The blanket was churning—arms, legs, shoes, and peanuts were flying all over the place.

I had to get the picture . . . fast! I rushed toward the body-mess and *blam!* I fell. "Ghost slime!" I screamed, pointing my flashlight to the white, goopy stuff on the floor.

"Willie! Hurry!" yelled Lucy. "I can't hold it much longer."

My hands were shaking and my fingers were slippery with sweat, but I aimed the camera. "Ready," I yelled.

Then everything happened at the same time. Lucy let go of the blanket. I snapped the flash camera. The ghost tore into me, screeching, clawing, biting. I was so busy fighting for my life I didn't see what Kyle and Lucy saw until I heard them yell.

"A PARROT!"

◆ 10 ◆

Beak-Bait

Lucy turned on the light. "A parrot!" I said, staring at a gray, feathered bird hanging from the curtain rod. "An African Gray. I took care of my cousin's last summer, and boy, did that bird like peanuts."

"That's what lured him out—your peanuts," said Lucy.

"*Eeeeerk!*" screeched the parrot. He was upside down, and his beak was open, ready to bite. He looked like a giant, bloodsucking bat.

"Look! I think he's shy," said Lucy, standing dangerously close to the blood-sucking bird.

"Are you crazy?" I said. "He's a monster! My cousin's bird was really mean. If you get too close he'll bite your hand off."

"I agree with Lucy," said Kyle. "I think he's shy."

Then Kyle did something really stupid. He started walking up to the parrot *with his hand out.*

"Beak-bait," I warned.

But Kyle kept going. He walked real slow and talked in a low voice. "Maybe when you want someone to be your friend you should talk softly so they know you really like them, even if they moved into your house."

When Kyle got closer, the parrot puffed up his feathers. Kyle kept talking in a soft, low voice until the parrot calmed down. When Kyle got real close, the parrot bent his head down, like he was going to lunge out and bite Kyle's hand off. Only he didn't. He stroked the top of his head against Kyle's hand.

"*Gotcha, Scarface,*" the parrot said.

"Hey," said Lucy, "I bet that's his name, Scarface."

"Hi, Scarface. How are ya doin'?" asked Kyle, softly.

Then Scarface—the big, mean, blood-sucking, hand-eating bird—just sort of melted. His feathers smoothed and he looked like he lost all the bones in his body. Then he oozed into Kyle's hand.

"*Love ya, Baby,*" said Scarface.

• 11 •

And Scarface

We met in Kyle's room a few days later. Lucy, Kyle, me, and Scarface.

"Hands up!" said Scarface. *"You have the right to remain silent."*

"Scarface is the best," I said.

"He's tough," said Lucy. "I mean, he's been alone in the attic for weeks, living off rainwater and birdseed."

Scarface smoothed his feathers, then reached over to Kyle's head and smoothed Kyle's hair.

"He knows a million words," Kyle said proudly.

"That's because he watched so many cop shows on TV with Loraine," said Lucy.

"*Ka-pow! Ka-pow-pow-pow!*" Scarface bounced up and down on Kyle's arm, making gunshot noises. Then, "*Aaauugh!*" he cried and went limp.

"His specialty is dying," said Kyle, stroking Scarface.

"Okay, but what are we going to do about *this?*" asked Lucy, tapping the notebook with her pencil. "The cover of our detective notebook is a mess."

We kept crossing out our names because we couldn't decide whose name to list first. Now there were ten crossed-out names. "I say we get a new book," I said.

"And a new name," said Lucy.

"Sure," said Kyle. "But let's keep it simple, like King Kyle and Associates."

"Forget it!" sputtered Lucy. "Lucky Lucy and Associates is way better. Who

wouldn't want a lucky detective agency?"

Kyle opened his mouth to say something. His face was red. I figured that in one second the Friend War would start again, so I held up my hands. "I think we need a title with none of our names in it."

"Okay," agreed Kyle.

"But it has to be catchy," said Lucy. "Like . . ."

"Gotcha, Scarface!" the parrot said.

"Scarface!" we all yelled out. "Scarface Detectives."

Scarface fluffed up his feathers. He liked the name, too.

Kyle got out a new notebook. None of the pages had been written on. Nothing had been crossed out. It was perfect. I wrote our new name on the cover.

Then we did this . . . dance. Well, it was kind of a dance. It was this sort of whooping, whoo-whoo-whooing, haunted house, ghostly dance. And the best part was, we all did it together. Me and my two best friends.

"Over my dead body!"

And Scarface.

WILLIE'S
HOUSE

LEAF
PILE